SHELDON'S LUNCH

To librarians, parents, and teachers:

Sheldon's Lunch is a Parents Magazine READ ALOUD Original — one title in a series of colorfully illustrated and fun-to-read stories that young readers will be sure to come back to time and time again.

Now, in this special school and library edition of *Sheldon's Lunch*, adults have an even greater opportunity to increase children's responsiveness to reading and learning — and to have fun every step of the way.

When you finish this story, check the special section at the back of the book. There you will find games, projects, things to talk about, and other educational activities designed to make reading enjoyable by giving children and adults a chance to play together, work together, and talk over the story they have just read.

For a free color catalog describing Gareth Stevens' list of high-quality books, call 1-800-542-2595 (USA) or 1-800-461-9120 (Canada). Gareth Stevens' Fax: (414) 225-0377.

Parents Magazine READ ALOUD Originals:

A Garden for Miss Mouse
Aren't You Forgetting
  Something, Fiona?
Bicycle Bear
The Biggest Shadow in
  the Zoo
Bread and Honey
Buggly Bear's Hiccup Cure
But No Elephants
Cats! Cats! Cats!
The Clown-Arounds
The Clown-Arounds Go
  on Vacation
Elephant Goes to School
The Fox with Cold Feet
Get Well, Clown-Arounds!
The Ghost in Dobbs Diner
The Giggle Book
The Goat Parade
Golly Gump Swallowed a Fly
Henry Babysits

Henry Goes West
Henry's Awful Mistake
Henry's Important Date
The Housekeeper's Dog
The Little Witch Sisters
The Man Who Cooked
  for Himself
Milk and Cookies
Miss Mopp's Lucky Day
No Carrots for Harry!
Oh, So Silly!
The Old Man and the
  Afternoon Cat
One Little Monkey
The Peace-and-Quiet Diner
Pets I Wouldn't Pick
Pickle Things
Pigs in the House
Rabbit's New Rug
Rupert, Polly, and Daisy
Sand Cake

Septimus Bean and His
  Amazing Machine
Sheldon's Lunch
Sherlock Chick and the
  Giant Egg Mystery
Sherlock Chick's First Case
The Silly Tail Book
Snow Lion
Socks for Supper
Sweet Dreams, Clown-
  Arounds!
Ten Furry Monsters
There's No Place Like Home
This Farm is a Mess
Those Terrible Toy-Breakers
Up Goes Mr. Downs
The Very Bumpy Bus Ride
Where's Rufus?
Who Put the Pepper in
  the Pot?
Witches Four

Library of Congress Cataloging-in-Publication Data

Lemerise, Bruce.
    Sheldon's lunch / by Bruce Lemerise.
      p. cm. -- (Parents magazine read aloud original)
    "North American library edition"--T.p. verso.
    Summary: Sheldon has more than enough pancakes for his own
  lunch but not enough for his friends, so they proceed to make more.
    ISBN 0-8368-0991-2
    [1. Pancakes, waffles, etc.--Fiction. 2. Cookery--Fiction.
  3. Animals--Fiction.] I. Title. II. Series.
  PZ7.L53737Sh 1994
  [E]--dc20   94-11355

This North American library edition published in 1994 by Gareth Stevens Publishing, 1555 North RiverCenter Drive, Suite 201, Milwaukee, Wisconsin, 53212, USA, under an arrangement with Pages, Inc., St. Petersburg, Florida.

Printed in the United States of America

1 2 3 4 5 6 7 8 9 9 99 98 97 96 95 94

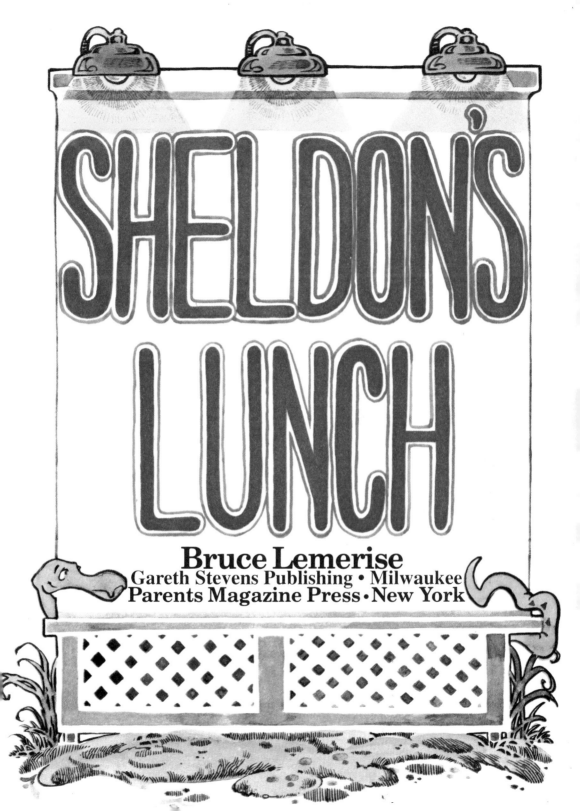

SHELDON'S LUNCH

Bruce Lemerise
Gareth Stevens Publishing • Milwaukee
Parents Magazine Press • New York

This book is dedicated to
my mother, MARIE LEMERISE,
who was always there
to fix my lunch.

Sheldon's mother was busy
making blueberry pancakes.
They were Sheldon's favorite.

Sheldon was playing
in the yard with his friends
when his mother called him
for lunch.

SHELDON,
LUNCH IS
READY!

"I have to go shopping," she said.
"Be good and clean up after
you're finished. Enjoy your lunch."

Sheldon sat down at the table.
He flipped pancakes one by one
in the air, catching them
in his mouth.

13

Suddenly, Sheldon heard a noise
behind him. He turned around
and saw his friends at the window.
"Mmm. Those pancakes look good,"
they said. "They probably
taste good, too."
There were more pancakes than
Sheldon could eat by himself,
so he invited his friends in.

They all began to eat.
"Blueberry pancakes are my favorite,"
said Oscar Raccoon.
"Mine, too," said Sheldon.

"I'm all finished, but I'm
still hungry," said Oscar.
"Me, too," said Randy Owl.
"More, please!" cried
Billy Frog and Chuck Bear.

"I've cooked many things,
but never pancakes," said Sheldon.
"They look easy enough, though."

Sheldon read from the cookbook.

Makes about twenty 2½-inch pancakes

2 cups all-purpose flour
1 teaspoon salt
1 teaspoon baking soda
2 eggs, slightly beaten
2 cups buttermilk
2 tablespoons melted butter or
    margarine
1 pint blueberries

Then he got to work.

Stir together the flour,
salt, and soda.
Add the eggs, milk, and butter.
Stir till just moist.
Mix in blueberries.

"Wait a minute," said Chuck.
"If blueberries are good
in pancakes, then how about
cinnamon, ginger, and honey?
I'm going to add some of each."

"This doesn't look like enough
batter," said Randy. "I think
it needs more flour and milk.
And I'll add some yeast, too.
That will make it grow!"

And then Oscar said,
"Don't forget marshmallows,
fudge, and cream!"

Billy looked on all the kitchen shelves
and came back with his arms full.
"I like a little bit of everything,"
he said.

The mixture began to grow

and grow.

The batter began to shake.

Then suddenly it spilled over
the edge of the bowl ...
all around the kitchen.
"Oh, no!" cried Randy.
"Look out!" yelled Sheldon.
"We're doomed!" screamed Oscar.

Everyone was covered from head to foot
in thick, gooey batter!

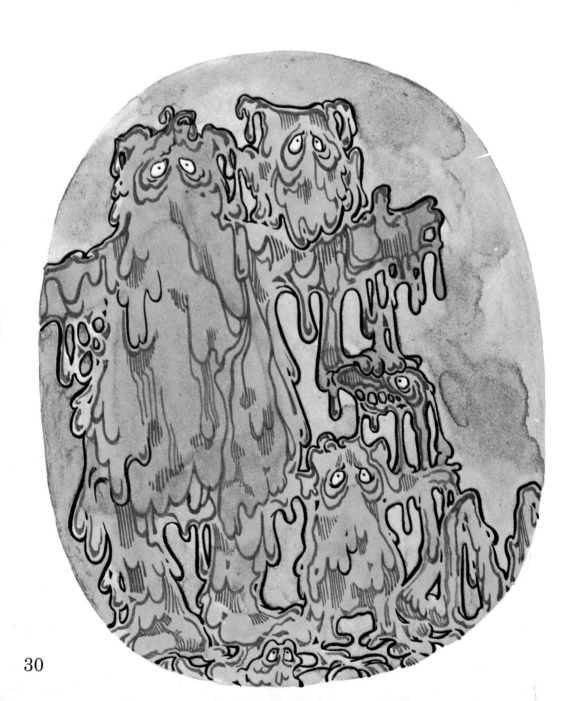

"Now we'll make pancakes
the right way," said Sheldon.
"First we'll clean ourselves up."
Sheldon was covered so thickly
that Oscar had to scrape
the batter off him.

"Now we'll clean up the mess!"
Sheldon continued.

Randy flapped about,
directing the clean-up.

Chuck scraped off batter
from all the high places.

Oscar scooped up batter
from all the low places.

Billy hopped around,
throwing away the garbage.

And Sheldon
swept,

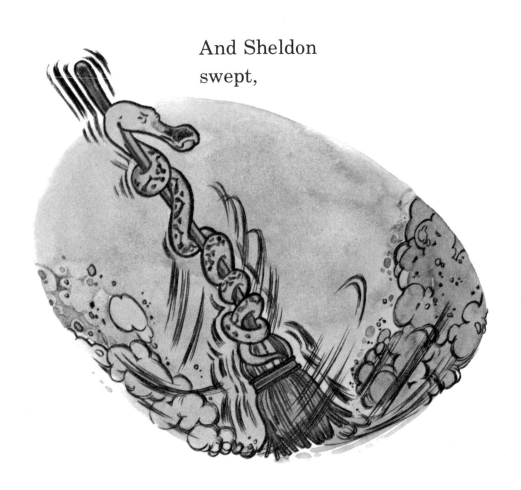

scrubbed,

and cleaned

until everything was spotless.

Sheldon and his friends had
all they wanted to eat.

And they all helped wash up.

Just as they finished,
Sheldon's mother
returned from shopping.

She put away her packages
and called to Sheldon
in the kitchen.
"Sheldon, did you have
a nice lunch?"

And Sheldon and his friends
called back ...

WE ALL HAD A
GREAT LUNCH!

PLEASE
TURN THE PAGE
FOR THE COMPLETE
RECIPE.

Makes about twenty 2½-inch pancakes

2 cups all-purpose flour
1 teaspoon salt
1 teaspoon baking soda
2 eggs, slightly beaten
2 cups buttermilk
2 tablespoons melted butter or
   margarine
1 pint blueberries

Stir together the flour,
salt, and soda.
Add the eggs, milk, and butter.

Stir till just moist.
Mix in blueberries.

Drop batter by scant 1/4 cupfuls
onto hot, lightly greased griddle.
(Don't crowd pancakes.)

Cook over medium heat
until top of pancake is bubbly
and bottom is golden brown.

Turn pancakes and brown other side.
(To flip pancakes, give turner
a sudden lift and tilt—
up and over!)

When pancakes are cooked,
keep them ready to eat by
placing them in shallow pan
in warm oven.

Make more pancakes using
rest of batter.

Notes to Grown-ups

Major Themes
Here is a quick guide to the significant themes and concepts at work in *Sheldon's Lunch*:

- Responsibility – it's fun for a child to have friends visit, but the child also needs to learn to be responsible for the guests' behavior. Following directions also has an important part in this story. The mess could have been avoided had the recipe been followed.
- Sharing – sharing enriches everyone's lives by helping people make friends and feel good about themselves.
- Cleanup – cleaning up a mess is easier if everyone pitches in to help.

Step-by-step Ideas for Reading and Talking
Here are some ideas for further give-and-take between grown-ups and children. The following topics encourage creative discussion of *Sheldon's Lunch* and invite the kind of open-ended response that is consistent with many contemporary approaches to reading, including Whole Language:

- What would your child have done in Sheldon's situation? Explain to your child what you would hope she or he would do in such a situation.
- Talk with your child about trust. Sheldon's mother trusted Sheldon at home by himself, but Sheldon got into trouble. Explain the importance of living up to someone's trust.
- Talk to your child about learning to say "no" when the situation calls for it. Sheldon could have respectfully said "no" to his friends and avoided the cooking mess completely.

Games for Learning

Games and activities can stimulate young readers and listeners alike to find out more about words, numbers, and ideas. Here are more ideas for turning learning into fun:

Make Your Own Cookbook

Cooking and baking help reinforce basic skills such as measuring, reading directions, and using simple math. Sheldon's comical catastrophe in the kitchen will remind your child of the importance of following directions in sequence.

Help your child record her or his version of several favorite recipes. For example, your child could probably tell you the main steps in preparing the dishes of a favorite meal, such as a Thanksgiving or birthday dinner. Write or type each recipe in large print on a large sheet of paper.

Your child may wish to illustrate the recipes, perhaps in the step-by-step format used by many basic cookbooks. By looking through cookbooks together, you can help your child notice and compare the different ways artwork is used to help explain a recipe. After punching holes and binding the tops or sides with yarn, you can add your original family cookbook to the rest in your collection!

Pancake Project

You and your child can make a special pancake breakfast together by following Sheldon's recipe and using your imaginations. Experiment with different pancake toppings, like applesauce or flavored syrups. Try adding different kinds of fruit to the pancakes, such as bananas or other types of berries. Use cookie cutters to make pancake animals or other shapes.

About the Author/Artist

BRUCE LEMERISE says, "As long as I can remember, I was interested in two things: drawing and snakes. As a boy, I went on snake hunts to find as many snakes as I could for my collection. At one time, I had ten garter snakes, a corn snake, a water snake, and a baby decay snake. I could never understand why people were afraid of them. Finally, owning a six-foot boa constrictor was a dream come true!"

Mr. Lemerise credits both his parents for getting him started in his career. Since art school, his work has included Broadway posters and greeting cards. This is his first children's book.